Finding
Perfect

Also by Colleen Hoover

Also by Colleen Hoover and Tarryn Fisher

Finding Perfect

A Novella

Colleen Hoover

**SIMON &
SCHUSTER**

London · New York · Sydney · Toronto · New Delhi

First published in the United States by Atria, 2018
First published in Great Britain by Simon & Schuster UK Ltd, 2022

3 5 7 9 10 8 6 4 2

Simon & Schuster UK Ltd
1st Floor
222 Gray's Inn Road
London WC1X 8HB

Simon & Schuster Australia, Sydney
Simon & Schuster India, New Delhi

www.simonandschuster.co.uk
www.simonandschuster.com.au
www.simonandschuster.co.in

A CIP catalogue record for this book
is available from the British Library

Paperback ISBN: 978-1-3985-2117-9
eBook ISBN: 978-1-3985-2118-6

Printed and bound by CPI Group (UK) Ltd, Croydon, CR0 4YY

MIX
Paper from
responsible sources
FSC® C171272

This is dedicated to Maggie.
You know what you did.

Note to the Reader

This novella focuses on characters in both *Finding Cinderella* and *All Your Perfects*. This will make more sense once you've read both of the novels that this novella ties together. For the best reading experience, the correct order is *Hopeless*, *Losing Hope*, *Finding Cinderella*, *All Your Perfects*, and then *Finding Perfect*. Please note that *All Your Perfects* can also be read as a standalone. Thank you and happy reading!

Finding Perfect

Chapter One

"That's three for me," Breckin says, dropping his Xbox controller. "I really need to go home now."

I pick up the controller and try to hand it back to him. "Just one more," I say. Or *beg*, really. But Breckin already has on his ridiculous puffy jacket and is making his way to my bedroom door.

"Call Holder if you're this bored," he says.

"He and Sky had Thanksgiving dinner at his dad's house yesterday. They won't be back until tonight."

"Then ask Six to come over. I've hung out with you enough today to last me until Christmas break. I have family shit tonight."

That makes me laugh. "You said *shit*."

Breckin shrugs. "Yeah. It's Thanksgiving. I have family shit."

"I thought Mormons couldn't swear."

Breckin rolls his eyes and opens my bedroom door. "Bye, Daniel."

"Wait. You coming Saturday?" On our drive home from school a couple days ago, Holder suggested we do a Friendsgiving while we're home on Thanksgiving break. Sky and Six are going to cook. *Which means we'll probably end up ordering pizza.*

"Yeah, I'll be there. But only if you stop pointing out my religious flaws."

"Deal. And I'll never call you Powder Puff again if you stay and play one more game with me."

Breckin looks bored with me. I don't blame him. I'm bored with myself.

"You need to go somewhere," he says. "You've been playing video games for twelve hours. It's starting to smell like a waffle cone in here."

"Why do you say that like it's a bad thing?"

"I meant it in a bad way." Breckin closes my bedroom door and I'm alone again.

So alone.

I fall back onto my bedroom floor and stare up at the ceiling for a while. Then I look at my phone and there's nothing. Six hasn't texted me at all today. I haven't texted her either, but I'm waiting for her to text me first. Things have been weird between us for the past couple months now. I was hoping it was because we were in a new setting, both in our first semesters of college, but she was quiet on the drive home, too.

She had family shit yesterday and hasn't even invited me over today.

I feel like she's about to break up with me.

I don't know why. I've never had a girl break up with me. I'm the one who broke up with Val, but I would think this is what it's like just before a breakup. Less communication. Less making time for each other. Less making out.

Maybe she does want to break up with me, but she knows it would hurt the awesome foursome we've got going on. We do everything with Sky and Holder now that we're all in college together. Breaking up with me would make it awkward for all three of them.

Maybe I'm overthinking things. Maybe it's college that's stressing her out.

My bedroom door opens and Chunk leans against the doorframe, arms folded. "Why are you on the floor?"

"Why are you in my room?"

She takes a step back so that she's technically in the hallway. "It's your turn to do the dishes."

"I don't even live here anymore."

"But you're home for Thanksgiving," she says. "Which means you're eating our food and using our dishes and sleeping under our roof, so go do the chores."

"You haven't changed at all."

"You moved out three months ago, Daniel. No one changes in the span of three months." Chunk walks back down the hallway without closing my door.

I have the urge to run after her and argue about people

not changing in just three months because Six has changed in that short of a time span. But if I disagree with her, I'll have to back it up with an example, and I'm not talking to Chunk about my girlfriend.

I check my phone one more time for a text from Six and then push myself off the floor. On my way to the kitchen, I pause at the doorway to Hannah's bedroom. She doesn't come home as often as I do because she goes to college in South Texas and is in med school.

I haven't even declared a major yet, nor have I found a job. That's not surprising, though. I haven't filled out a single application.

Hannah is sitting up in bed with her laptop. Probably doing homework for med school or something equally responsible. "Do they still make you do dishes when you come home?" I ask her.

She glances up at me before looking back down at her computer screen. "No. I don't live here anymore."

I knew she was the favorite. "Then why do *I* have to do chores?"

"Mom and Dad still support you financially. You owe them."

That's a fair point. I remain in her doorway, stalling the inevitable. "What are you doing?"

"Homework," she says.

"Want to take a break and play video games with me?"

Hannah looks up at me like I've suggested she murder someone. "Have I *ever* wanted to play video games with you?"

I groan. "Ugh." *This is going to be a long week.*

Holder and Sky get back tonight, but they're busy until Saturday. Breckin has family shit. I can already feel the unavoidable heartbreak coming from Six, which is why I've avoided her all day. I really don't want to be dumped over Thanksgiving break. Or at all. Maybe if I never text or call or speak to Six again, she'll never be able to break up with me and then I can continue to live in my blissful ignorance.

I push off Hannah's door and head toward the kitchen when she calls for me to come back. I turn around in the hallway, my whole body floppy and defeated when I reappear in her doorway.

"What's wrong with you?" she asks.

My shoulders are sagging and I'm in the midst of feeling really sorry for myself, so I sigh dramatically. "Everything."

Hannah motions toward the beanbag chair across the bedroom. I walk over to it and plop down. I don't know why I'm allowing her to summon me into her room, because she's just going to ask questions I don't want to answer. But it makes me a little less bored than I've been all day. And, also, it beats doing the dishes.

"Why are you moping? Did you and Six break up?" she asks.

"Not yet, but it feels imminent."

"Why? What'd you do wrong?"

"Nothing," I say defensively. "At least I don't remember doing anything. I don't know, it's complicated. Our whole relationship is complicated."

Hannah laughs and closes her laptop. "Med school is complicated. Relationships are easy. You love a person; they love you back. If that's not how your relationship is, you end it. Simple."

I shake my head in disagreement. "But I do love Six and she does love me and it's still very, very complicated."

Sometimes Hannah gets this look of excitement in her eyes, but it seems to happen at the worst moments. Like right now, as I tell her my relationship may be doomed.

That shouldn't excite her. "Maybe I can help," she says.

"You can't help."

Hannah hops off her bed and walks to her bedroom door and shuts it. She turns around and faces me, her eyebrows narrowed, the excitement in her expression gone. "You haven't made me laugh since I got home. Something is changing you, and as your big sister, I want to know what it is. And if you don't tell me, I'll call a Wesley family meeting."

"You wouldn't." I hate those meetings. They always seem to be an intervention for me and my behavior when they're supposed to be about the entire family.

"Try me," Hannah says.

I groan and cover my face with both hands as I bury myself deeper into the beanbag. In all honesty, Hannah is the best voice of reason in our whole family. She might even be the *only* voice of reason. Chunk is too young to understand these issues. My father is too immature, like me. And my mother would flip out if I told her about Six and my truth.

I do want to talk about it, and Hannah is probably the only person in the world besides Sky and Holder who I would trust with this. But Sky and Holder don't talk about it because we made them pinky swear they'd never bring it up.

I'm scared if I don't talk to someone about it, Six and I will be over. And I can't imagine a life without Six in it now that I've had a life with Six in it.

I blow out a conceding breath. "Okay. But sit down first."

The excitement in her expression returns. She doesn't just sit down on her bed. She hops onto her bed, next to a lump of covers, and sits cross-legged, eager to hear what I'm about to tell her. She rests her chin in her hand, waiting.

I take a moment to figure out how to start the conversation. How to summarize it without going into too much detail.

"This sounds crazy," I say, "but I had sex with a girl in the maintenance closet during junior year of high school. I didn't know who she was or what she looked like because it was dark."

"That doesn't sound crazy," Hannah interjects. "That sounds exactly like something you would do."

"No, that's not the crazy part. The crazy part is that after I got with Six, I found out that *she* was the girl I had sex with in the closet. And . . . well . . . I got her pregnant. And because she didn't know who I was, she put the baby up for adoption. A closed adoption. So, I'm a dad, but I'm not.

And Six is a mom, but she's not. And we thought it would be okay and we'd be able to move past it, but we can't. She's sad all the time. And because *she's* sad all the time, *I'm* sad all the time. And when we're together, we're double sad, so we don't even really hang out all that much anymore. Now I think she's about to break up with me."

I feel protected by the beanbag right now because my gaze is on the ceiling and not on Hannah. I don't want to look at her after vomiting all that. But an entire minute goes by and neither of us says anything, so I finally lower my head.

Hannah is sitting as still as a statue, staring at me in shock, like I've just told her I got someone pregnant. Because I did. And that's apparently very shocking, which is why she's looking at me like this.

I give her another moment to let it sink in. I know she wasn't expecting to find out she's sort of an aunt with a nephew she'll never meet during a conversation she probably expected to be about something a lot more trivial, like miscommunication with my girlfriend.

"Wow," she says. "That's . . . *wow*. That's really complicated, Daniel."

"Told you so."

The room is silent. Hannah shakes her head in disbelief. She opens her mouth a couple of times to speak, but then shuts it.

"So, what do I do?" I ask.

"I have no idea."

I throw my hands up in defeat. "I thought you were going to *help* me. That's why I told you all that."

"Well, I was wrong. This is like . . . *severe* adult shit. I'm not there yet."

I drop my head back against the beanbag. "You suck as a big sister."

"Not as much as you suck at being a boyfriend."

Why does any of that make me suck? I sit up straight now and scoot to the edge of the beanbag. "Why? What did I do wrong?"

She waves her hand at me. "*This.* You're avoiding her."

"I'm giving her space. That's different."

"How long have things been weird between you?"

I think back on the months we've been together. "It was great when we first got together. But when I found out what had happened, it got weird for like a day, but we moved past it. Or I *thought* we did. But she always has this sadness about her. I see it a lot. Like she's forcing herself to pretend to be happy. It's just getting worse, though, and I don't know if it's college or me or everything she went through. But I noticed in October she started making more and more excuses not to hang out. She had a test, or a paper, or she was tired. So, then *I* started making excuses because I thought that if she doesn't want to hang out with me, I don't want to force her to."

Hannah is listening intently to every word I say. "When was the last time you kissed her?" she asks.

"Yesterday. I still kiss her and treat her the same when we're together. It's just . . . different. We're hardly together."

She lifts a shoulder. "Maybe she feels guilty."

"I know she does, and I've tried to tell her she made the right choice."

"Then maybe she just wants to forget it ever happened, but you ask her too many questions about it."

"I don't ask her *any*. I never ask her. She doesn't seem to want to talk about it, so we don't."

Hannah tilts her head. "She carried your child for nine months and then put it up for adoption and you haven't asked her questions about it?"

I shrug. "I *want* to. I just . . . don't want her to feel pressured to relive it."

Hannah makes a groaning sound like I just said something that disappoints her.

"What?"

She looks at me pointedly. "I have never liked a single girl you've dated until Six. Please go fix this."

"How?"

"*Talk* to her. Be there for her. Ask her questions. Ask her what you can do to make it better for her. Ask her if it would help her to talk about it with you."

I chew on that suggestion. It's good advice. I don't know why I haven't just straight-up asked her how I can help make it better for her. "I don't know why I haven't done that yet," I admit.

"Because you're a guy and that's not your fault. It's Dad's fault."

Hannah might actually be right. Maybe the only problem between Six and me right now is that I'm a guy and guys are dumb. I push myself out of the beanbag. "I'm gonna go over there."

"Don't get her fucking pregnant again, you idiot."

I nod, but I don't go into detail with Hannah about the fact that Six and I haven't had sex since we've officially been a couple. That's no one's business but ours.

The one time we had sex was honestly the greatest sex I've ever had. If she breaks up with me, we won't get to experience that again. I've thought about what it'll be like so much, in such extensive detail, I'm confident it would be damn near perfect. Now I'm even more bummed by our prospective breakup. Not only will I have to spend my life without Six, I'll also have to spend the rest of my life never being interested in sex again, since it won't be with Six. Sex with Six is the only sex I'm willing to entertain. She's ruined me forever.

I open Hannah's door to leave.

"Do the dishes first," Chunk says with a muffled voice.

Chunk?

I turn around, inspecting Hannah's room, looking for where Chunk might be hiding. I walk over to the pile of covers on Hannah's bed and pull them back. Chunk is lying there with a pillow over her head.

What in the hell? I point to Chunk while looking at Hannah. "She's been here this whole time?"

"Yeah," Hannah says with a careless shrug. "I thought you knew."

I run my hands over my face. "Christ. Mom and Dad are gonna *kill* me."

Chunk tosses the pillow aside and rolls over to look up at me. "I can keep a secret, you know. I've matured since you moved out."

"You literally just told me ten minutes ago that no one can change in a span of three months."

"That was ten minutes ago," she says. "People can change in a span of three months and ten minutes."

There's no way she's going to be able to keep this quiet. I should never have said anything to either of them. I throw the covers back over Chunk and make my way to the door. "If either of you tell Mom and Dad about this, I'll never speak to you again."

"That's an incentive, not a threat," Chunk says.

"Then I'll move back home if you tell them!"

"My lips are sealed," she says.

Chapter Two

It's been a long time since I've knocked on Six's bedroom window.

She and Sky share a dorm on campus now, but it's on the fifth floor of a building and I can't climb that high. I tried a few weeks ago because our dorm curfew is ten o'clock, but it was almost midnight and I really wanted to see Six. I got scared halfway up to the first floor and climbed back down.

I glance at Sky's bedroom window, but the lights are out. I guess she and Holder haven't made it back from Austin yet. When I look at Six's window, her lights are out, too. I hope she's home. She didn't mention she was going anywhere.

But then again, I haven't asked her. I never ask her anything. I hope Hannah is right and I can somehow fix whatever is weird between us.

I knock quietly on the windowpane, hoping she's in her

room. I immediately hear movement and then her curtains are pushed aside.

She looks like a fucking angel. Still.

I wave at her and she smiles at me. She actually looks happy to see me. That smile eliminates the majority of my nerves.

This always happens. I get paranoid and worried when I'm away from her, but when I'm with her, I can still see how she feels about me. Even when she looks sad.

Six opens the window so I can climb inside. Her bedroom is dark, like she's been sleeping, but it's only nine o'clock.

I turn to face her and take her in. She's wearing a T-shirt and pajama bottoms plastered with pizza slices. It reminds me that I haven't eaten dinner today. I don't even remember eating lunch. I haven't had much of an appetite.

"What's up?" she asks.

"Nothing."

She stares at me for a moment and then gets this look in her eyes like she's uncomfortable. She walks to her bed and sits down. She pats the spot next to her, so I lie down and stare up at her.

"I lied," I say. "It isn't nothing."

Six sighs heavily and then scoots down so that she's lying down next to me. She doesn't turn toward me, though. She stares up at the ceiling. "I know."

"You do?"

She nods. "I was expecting you to show up tonight."

I'm suddenly regretting coming over here and confronting it, because confronting it means action will be taken, and it might not be an action I want. *Shit. Now I'm scared.* "Are you breaking up with me?" I ask her.

She rolls her head and looks at me sincerely. "No, Daniel. Don't be a dumbass. Why? Are you breaking up with me?"

"No," I say immediately. Convincingly. "Dumbass."

She laughs a little. That's a good sign, but she looks away again, back to the ceiling, and offers up nothing else.

"Why are things weird between us?" I ask her.

"I don't know," she answers quietly. "I've been wondering the same thing."

"What am I doing wrong?"

"I don't know."

"But *am* I doing something wrong?" I ask.

"I don't know."

"What can I do to be better?"

"I don't even know if you can *be* any better."

"Well, if I'm not the issue, what is?"

"Everything else? Nothing else? I don't know."

"This conversation isn't going anywhere," I say.

She smiles. "Yeah, we've never been the best at deep conversation."

We aren't. We're shallow. Both of us. Our conversations are mostly shallow. We like to keep things fun and light because everything under the surface is so damn heavy. "That doesn't seem to be working out for us too well, so tell me what you're thinking. Let's dig a little and figure this out."

Six turns her head and eyes me. "I'm thinking about how much I hate the holidays," she says.

"Why? They're the best. No classes, lots of food; we get to sit around and be fat and lazy."

She doesn't laugh. She just looks sad. And then it hits me why she hates the holidays, and I feel like an idiot. I want to apologize but I don't know how. So instead, I slip my fingers through hers and squeeze her hand. "Do holidays make you think about him?"

She nods. "Always."

I don't know what to say to that. While I'm trying to think of a way to make her feel better, she rolls onto her side and faces me.

I let go of her hand and reach up to her cheek, stroking it with my thumb. Her eyes are so sad, and I want to kiss her eyelids, as if it'll make that look go away. It won't. It's always there, hidden behind fake smiles.

"Do you ever think about him?" she asks.

"Yes," I admit. "Not in the way you do, I'm sure. You carried him for nine months. Loved him. Held him. I didn't know about him until I already knew the outcome, so I don't think it left as big of a hole in me as it did in you."

A single tear rolls down her cheek, and while I'm glad we're talking about this, I'm also very, very sad for her. I think this has affected her a lot more than I realized.

"I wish I could make it better for you," I say, pulling her against my chest. I always try to use humor to fix the sad things, but humor can't fix this and it's all I know. "It scares me because I don't know how to make you happy."

"I'm scared I'll always be sad."

I'm scared she'll always be sad, too. And, of course, I would take whatever version of Six I can get, whether that's happy or sad or mad, but for her sake, I want her to be happy. I want her to forgive herself. I want her to stop worrying.

It's a while before she starts talking again. And when she does, her voice is shaking. "It feels like . . ." She sighs heavily before she continues. "It's like someone took a huge chunk out of my chest and there are two parts of me now that don't connect. I feel so disconnected, Daniel."

Her painful admission makes me wince. I kiss the top of her head and just hold her. I don't know what to say that'll make her feel better. I never know what to say. Maybe that's why I don't ask her about him, because I feel like she carries all the burden and I don't know how to lift it off of her.

"Does it help you to talk about it?" I ask her. "Because you never do."

"I didn't think you wanted to know."

"I do. I just didn't think you wanted to talk about it. But I do want to know. I want to know everything if you feel like telling me."

"I don't know. It might make me feel worse, but I do sometimes want to tell you about it all."

"Then tell me. What was it like? The pregnancy?"

"Scary. I hardly left my host family's house. I think

I was depressed, now that I look back on it. I didn't want anyone to know, not even Sky, because I had already made up my mind that I would put him up for adoption before I came back. So, I kept it all to myself and didn't tell anyone back home because I thought it would make the decision more bearable if no one else knew about it. I thought it was a brave choice at the time, but now I wonder if it was a scared choice."

I pull back and look her in the eyes. "It was both. You were scared *and* you were brave. But most of all, you were selfless."

That makes her smile. Maybe I'm actually doing something right here. I think of more questions to ask her. "How did you find out you were pregnant? Who was the first person you told?"

"I was late for my period, but I thought it might have been the travel and being in an entirely foreign situation. But when I didn't get it the second time, I bought a test. I took it and it wasn't one of those plus or minus sign tests. It was the kind that said "pregnant" or "not pregnant," but it was in Italian. It said "*incinta.*" I had no idea what that meant, and I had taken the test at school, so I couldn't use my phone to google it because it was in my locker. So, after my last class, I asked the American teacher at my school what *incinta* meant, and when she said, "pregnant," I started crying. So . . . I guess Ava was technically the first person I told."

"How did she react?"

"She was amazing. I really liked her, and for the first month, she was the only one I told. She went over all my options with me. She even came with me when I told my host family. And she never made me feel pressured, so it was nice to have her to talk to. When I decided on adoption, she said she knew a couple who was looking to adopt, but they wanted a closed adoption because they were scared I would change my mind in the future. But Ava vouched for them and I trusted her, so she helped us get a lawyer and was by my side through the whole process. And even though she knew the host family, she never tried to get them to persuade her decision."

I don't want to interrupt her, because I've been wanting to know all of this since the day I found out she'd had a baby, but I can't get past the tidbit of information Six just shared. "Wait," I say. "This teacher. She knows who adopted the baby? Can't we reach out to her?"

Six looks deflated when I ask that. She shakes her head. "I agreed to the closed adoption. We all signed legal paperwork. And despite all that, I've called her twice since I've been back, begging her for information. Her hands are tied. Legally and ethically. It's a dead end, Daniel. I'm sorry."

I deflate at that news but try not to show it. I nod and kiss her forehead reassuringly. I feel stupid even assuming she hadn't tried that avenue already. I feel stupid that I haven't tried any avenue *at all*. I haven't even offered. Now that I'm looking at this situation as a whole, I'm surprised she still puts up with me.

I keep her talking so she can't focus on the same thing I'm focused on—how much I suck.

"What was the delivery like?"

"Hurt like hell, but it went pretty quick. They let me keep him in my room for an hour. It was just me and him. I cried the whole time. And I almost changed my mind, Daniel. I almost did. But it wasn't because I thought he'd be better off with me. It was because I didn't want to hurt. I didn't want to miss him. I didn't want to feel the emptiness I knew I was going to feel. But I knew if I kept him, it would just be for selfish reasons. I was worried how it would affect *me*." She wipes at her eyes before continuing. "Before they came and got him, I looked down at him and said, '*I'm not doing this because I don't love you. I'm doing it because I do.*' That was the only thing I said to him out loud before they came for him. I wish I would have said more."

I can feel tears stinging my own eyes. I just pull her closer to me. I can't imagine what that was like for her. I can't imagine how much pain she's been in this whole time. I can't believe I thought it was because of me. I'm not significant enough to cause someone the kind of pain having to say goodbye to your own child causes.

"After the nurse took him away, she came back to my room and sat with me while I cried. She said, '*I know this is the worst day of your life. But thanks to you, it just became the best day of two other people's lives.*'" Six inhales a shaky breath. "It made me feel a little better in that moment. Like maybe she saw adoptions happen a lot and she knew it was hard for me. It helped me realize I wasn't the only mother giving up her child."

I shake my head adamantly. "You didn't *give him up*, Six. I hate that phrase. You gave him a life. And you gave his new parents a life. The last thing you did was give up. You *stood up*."

That makes her cry. Hard. She curls into me and I just hold her, running my hand gently over her head. "I know it's scary because we don't know what kind of life he has, but you don't know what kind of life he would have had if you had kept him. And you'd have the same kind of doubts if you had made that choice, too—wondering if you should have given him to someone in a position to care for him. There's so much unknown to swim around in and that'll probably always be there. You might always feel disconnected. But you have me. I know I can't change what you went through in the past, but I *can* make you promises. And I can keep them."

She lifts her face from my chest and looks up at me with red eyes and a little bit of hope. "What kind of promises?"

I brush hair away from her face. "I promise that I will never doubt your decision," I say. "I promise I will never talk about it unless you feel like talking about it. I promise I'll keep trying to make you smile, even when I know it's the kind of sadness that a joke can't fix. I promise to always love you, no matter what." I press my lips against hers and kiss her, then pull back. "No matter *what*, Six. *No. Matter. What.*"

Her eyes are still full of tears and I know her heart is still full of sadness, but through it all, she smiles at me. "I don't deserve you, Daniel."

"I know," I say in complete agreement. "You deserve someone way better."

She laughs, and the sound of it makes my heart swell.

"I guess I'm stuck with you until someone better comes along, then."

I smile back at her, and finally, *finally*, things feel normal again. As normal as things can be between people like Six and me.

"I love you, Cinderella," I whisper.

"I love you, too. No matter what."

Chapter Three

When I got home from Six's house last night, I slept through the night for the first time in a month. I went to bed relieved that we were okay.

But I woke up this morning feeling *not* okay.

Sure, our relationship finally seems stable. But Six is hurting. A lot. And I keep telling myself there's nothing I can do, but when I woke up feeling unsettled, I realized it's because I haven't even been trying. Sure, it was a closed adoption. Sure, I'll probably keep getting doors slammed in my face. But what kind of boyfriend would I be if I didn't at least try to make Six's world better?

This is why I've been on the phone for two hours. I called seven adoption agencies and was told the same thing from each of them. They aren't allowed to release any information. I keep trying, though, because what if I get the one person who is a little bit unethical in my favor?

I was on the eighth phone call when Hannah walked in. I told her all about my conversation with Six and how I feel like I should be doing more to try to find out information about who might have our son, or if someone can just tell us he's okay.

I told Chunk, too, because she's Hannah's shadow every time Hannah's home from med school.

I debated not updating them, because I really don't want them to talk about it at all, ever, but it's also nice to have people who know the truth. And besides, three brains are better than one, even if they're all Wesley brains.

Hannah has called three lawyers in Italy so far. Two immediately told her no, there's nothing they can do to help. She's on the phone with the third one now.

"Adoption," she says, googling something. "Um. Italian. *Adozione*?" She waits for a moment, and then looks down at the phone with a defeated expression. "He hung up on me."

Every phone call leaves me a little more disappointed than the last.

"Someone has to be able to help," Hannah says. She falls back onto my bed, just as frustrated as I am.

Chunk is seated in my desk chair, spinning in a circle. "What if you're kicking a hornet's nest?" she says. "I mean, there was a reason they wanted a closed adoption. They don't want you guys involved."

"Yeah, because they were scared Six would come back to take her baby," I say. "But she won't. She just wants to know he's okay."

"I think you need to leave it be," Chunk says.

I look at Hannah, hoping she doesn't feel the same way.

"I'm usually on Chunk's side, but I'm actually on your side this time," Hannah says to me. "Keep pushing. Maybe ask Six more questions. Someone has to know something. Italy isn't that big, is it?"

"Sixty million people live in Italy," I say. "Even if we contacted forty people a day, it would take us over four thousand years to make it through everyone in Italy."

Hannah laughs. "You actually did the math?"

I nod pathetically.

"Well, shit," she mutters. "I don't know. You just have to keep trying. Maybe the host family knows who it was."

I shake my head. "Six said they weren't really involved. There was an American teacher who worked at the school who helped Six with the adoption. I asked Six if there was a way to get in touch with her, but Six has already tried to get information from her on more than one occasion. The woman refuses to share anything based on legal grounds."

Hannah looks hopeful. "But this woman knows? Does anyone know where she might be?"

I shrug. "I don't know *what* she knows, exactly. I just know she helped Six."

"Call her," Hannah says.

"No."

"Why not?"

"Because Six said she's tried that already. More than once. The woman is a brick wall."

"But you're annoying. It might work for you."

Should I be offended by that? "What does me being annoying have to do with it?"

Hannah picks up my phone and puts it back in my hand. "You have to be persistent to be annoying. Be persistent with her."

I look at my phone. "I don't even know who to call. I don't know what school it was."

Hannah asks for the name of the city where Six did her foreign exchange, and then writes down three numbers as she searches the internet. I can't remember the name of the woman Six said she knew, but I do remember she said she was American. I call the first two schools and ask if they have an American teacher on the faculty and both say no.

I dial the third number with little hope left.

A woman answers in Italian.

"Do you speak English?" I ask her.

"Yes. How can I help you?"

"I'm looking for a teacher. An American teacher. I can't remember her name, but I need to speak to her."

"We have one American teacher on staff. Ava Roberts."

"Ava!" I yell. *That's it!* That's the name Six mentioned last night. "Yes," I say, trying to calm myself. I'm standing now and I don't even remember standing up. I clear my throat. "May I please speak to Ava Roberts?"

"One moment." I'm placed on hold and my heart is pounding. I use my T-shirt to wipe sweat from my forehead.

"What's happening?" Chunk asks, appearing a little more interested.

"I'm on hold. But I think this is the right school."

Hannah brings her hands to her mouth right when someone picks up on the other end. "Ava Roberts, how can I help you?"

My voice is shaking when I start to speak. "Hi. Hello." I clear my throat again. "My name is Daniel Wesley."

"Ah, a fellow American," she says. *She sounds friendly.* "Are you wanting to sign up as an exchange student?"

"No. No, I'm in college. I'm calling about something else. It might be weird, I don't know."

There's a pause. "Okay," she says, drawing the word out. I hear the sound of a door close, as if she's giving this conversation privacy. "What can I help you with?"

"Um. Do you remember a student by the name of Six Jacobs? Or maybe she went by Seven Jacobs?"

The lack of reply on her end gives me my answer. She definitely knows who I'm talking about. It doesn't mean I'll get any answers, but it feels good to know I'm on the right track.

"Daniel, you said?"

"Yes, ma'am."

"Daniel, I hope you understand that I'm not allowed to discuss students in any capacity. Is there anything else I can help you with?"

She knows. She knows why I'm calling. I can hear the fear in her voice.

"Don't hang up," I beg. "Please. I just. Okay, so I'm going to go out on a limb here and assume you're the teacher who helped Six with the adoption. She mentioned you knew a couple who was looking to adopt, which means you might still know the couple. Which means you're the only living person I've been in touch with who can tell us where our baby is."

More heart-pounding silence. "Why are you calling me? I'm not allowed to discuss this."

"We just want to know that he's okay."

"It was a closed adoption, Daniel. I'm sorry. I can't legally discuss this with anyone."

"I know." My voice is desperate. I'm scared she's about to hang up, so I just start talking faster, hoping to get it all out before she does. "We know you can't discuss it. We aren't asking for contact. And I'm not calling because we want him back. I mean, if he's not in a good situation, we do, but if he's happy and his parents are happy, that'll make *us* happy. We just . . ." I feel out of my element. Nervous. Like I don't know how to ask this woman for a morsel of information. But then I think about what Hannah said. She's right. I *am* annoying. I'm persistent. I blow out a breath and continue. "She cries, you know. Every night. It's the not knowing that kills her. I don't know if you have a way of contacting the people who adopted him, but if you do, maybe they wouldn't mind just sending her an email. An update. Even if *you* just respond with one sentence saying he's fine, I'm sure that would mean the world to Six. That's all I'm asking for. Just . . . it's hard, you know? Not knowing. It's really hard on her."

There's a long silence. *Such* a long silence. I'm worried

she hung up, so I look down at the phone, but it still says the call is connected. I put it on speaker and wait. Then I hear something that sounds like a sniffle come from the phone.

Is she crying?

Hannah and I lock eyes, and I know my expression must match the shock on her face.

"I can't make any promises," Ava says. "I can reach out to the adoption agency with your message. Email me your contact information, but . . . don't get your hopes up, Daniel. Please. All I can do is try to get a message to them. I can't promise they'll receive it or that they'll even feel comfortable answering it if they do."

I frantically point at my desk, motioning for Chunk to get me a pen and paper. "Okay." I sound so desperate, I know. "Thank you. *Thank you.* You have no idea what this means to me. To us."

"You already sound excited," the woman says. "I told you not to get your hopes up."

I grip the back of my neck. "Sorry. I'm not excited. I mean, I am. But a realistic excited."

"Do you have a pen?" she asks. She already sounds full of regret for even agreeing to do this, but I don't care how much regret she feels. I feel no shame.

I take down her email address and thank her two more times. When I hang up, Hannah and Chunk and I stare at each other.

I think I might be in shock. I can't form any words, or even much of a thought.

This is the first time I've ever been grateful for being called annoying.

"Wow," Chunk says. "What if it works?"

Hannah presses her hands to the sides of her head. "Oh my God. I honestly didn't think we'd get anywhere."

I let it all out by punching the air with my fists. I want to scream, but Mom and Dad are here in the house somewhere. I pull Hannah and Chunk in for a hug and we start jumping up and down. Hannah starts squealing because that's what she does when she's excited, but it actually doesn't annoy me this time.

"What the hell is going on?"

We all separate immediately. My father is standing in the doorway, looking at us suspiciously.

"Nothing," we all say in unison.

He cocks an eyebrow. "Bullshit."

I put one arm around Hannah's shoulders and one arm around Chunk's. "I just missed my sisters, Dad."

He points at us. "Bullshit," he says again.

My mother is behind him now. "What's wrong?"

"They were happy," my father says, accusatory.

My mother looks at him like he's lost his mind. "What do you mean?"

He motions toward us. "They were hugging and squealing. Something is up."

My mother is looking at us suspiciously now. "You were hugging? Like all three of you?" She folds her arms across her chest. "You three never hug. What the hell is going on?"

Hannah walks toward the door and smiles at my parents. "With all due respect," she says, "this is none of your business." Then she closes the door in their faces.

I can't believe she just did that.

She locks the door, and when she looks back at Chunk and me, we all just start laughing, and then we hug again and resume our celebratory moment.

My parents don't knock. I think we've thoroughly confused them.

Hannah falls onto the bed. "Are you telling Six?"

"No," I say immediately. "I don't want to get her hopes up. We may never hear from them."

"I bet you do," Chunk says.

"I hope so. But like you said, there's a reason they chose a closed adoption."

"Yeah," she says. "The waiting is going to suck."

It really is going to suck. I sit down on my bed and think about how much it's going to suck. Especially if I never hear back from anyone.

I hope she knows I'll be calling her again next week. And the week after that. And the week after that. I'll call her until she changes her number or her name.

But if either of those things happen, I'll be back to square one.

Now that the energy is leaving the room, the reality of it all begins to sink in. The three of us grow quiet in the midst of our declining hope.

"Well," Hannah says. "If you never hear from them,

you could always do one of those online DNA tests and hope your child does one when they're older, too. There's always that."

"Yeah, but then Daniel would never be able to commit a murder," Chunk says. "His DNA would always be in the system." Hannah and I both look at her. Chunk shrugs off our wary looks. "I just wouldn't take that chance."

Hannah and I continue to stare at her. "You scare me," I say.

"Not as much as the idea of you being a dad scares *me*," Chunk retorts. Loudly.

I cover her mouth with my hand, staring at the door to my bedroom. "Shh. They could still be at the door," I whisper. I slowly release my hand from her mouth.

Hannah pipes up from her position on the bed. "Oh, man. I didn't think about that. If this works out, you're gonna *have* to tell Mom and Dad."

I didn't think about that, either. But finding out even the most insignificant information for Six would be worth my parents' anger.

Chunk starts giggling. "Dude, you're gonna be in *so* much trouble."

Hannah laughs, too. I glare at her because I thought we were on the same team, but that cruel excitement is back in her eyes.

"You know," I say, "for a moment there, I felt like the three of us bonded. But now I see that the two of you still find pleasure in the idea of my failure."

I open the door and motion for them to leave my room. "You can go now. You two are no longer needed here."

Hannah hops off the bed and grabs Chunk's hand, pulling her out of the chair. "We want this to work out for you, Daniel," Hannah says on her way out the door. "But we also look forward to shit hitting the fan when Mom and Dad find out."

"Yes," Chunk agrees. "Looking very forward to that."

I close the door and lock them out of my bedroom.

Chapter Four

We decided on Sky's house for our Friendsgiving because Karen and Jack will be gone most of the day. Six recruited me to help make the dressing, but I've never cooked in my life, so I've been more of a nuisance than a help. Sky is doing the baking because she makes the best cookies in the world, according to Holder.

When I drop the second egg in two minutes, Six finally regrets her choice. "Just go hang out with Holder and Breckin in the living room," she says. "I feel like it'll be easier without you in the kitchen."

I don't take any offense because it's the truth.

I go to the living room and sit next to Breckin. He's playing a video game with Holder. "You winning, Powder Puff?"

He lazily turns his head and looks at me, annoyed. "We went an entire week without you calling me that. I thought you actually learned something in college."

"What could I learn that would make me stop calling you Powder Puff?"

"Oh, I don't know. Decency?"

Holder laughs from the recliner he's sprawled out in. I glare in his direction. "What are you laughing at, Pimple Dick?"

"Breckin's right," Holder says. "Sometimes I think maybe you're maturing, but then you go and say something ignorant again to set me straight. Still the same ol' Daniel."

I shake my head. "I thought that was why you like me, because I don't change. I'm myself all the time."

"I think that's the problem," Breckin says. "You don't evolve. But you're getting better. I haven't heard you use the *R* word in a derogatory way since you've been home."

"What's the *R* word?" I ask. I have no idea what he's talking about.

He begins to spell it out for me. "R-E-T-A-R—"

I cut Breckin off. "Oh. That," I say. "Yeah, I learned not to say that when a chick in my economics class smacked me in the back of the head with her notebook."

"Maybe there's hope for you yet," Breckin says. "Come to think of it, I did seem to hate you a lot more in high school. But I wouldn't hate you at all if you'd stop calling me Powder Puff."

"Aren't you on Twitter?" Holder asks. "Don't you see what happens to people like you?"

"People like me?"

"Yeah. Guys who say insensitive shit because they think it makes them look cool and careless."

"I don't think I'm cool and careless. I just had no idea Powder Puff was insensitive."

"Bullshit," Holder says with a fake cough.

"Okay, so maybe I knew it was insensitive," I admit, looking back at Breckin. "But it's a joke."

"Well," Breckin says, "as someone who identifies as a gay male, I feel it's my duty to teach you how to be more sensitive. Powder Puff is insulting. So is the *R* word. And *most* of the nicknames you give to people."

"Yeah," Holder says. "Stop calling my girlfriend Cheese Tits."

"But . . . it's a joke. I don't even know what Cheese Tits or Powder Puff mean."

Holder turns his head and looks at me. "I know you don't. Neither do I. But Breckin is right. You're an asshole sometimes, and you should stop being an asshole sometimes."

Shit. I seem to be learning a lot of what people think about me over Thanksgiving break, whether I want to or not. So far, I've learned I'm insensitive. I'm an asshole. I'm annoying. I'm a guy. *What else is wrong with me?*

"That means I have to come up with a new nickname for you," I say to Breckin.

"You could just call me Breckin."

I nod. "I will. For now."

That seems to satisfy him. I lean back, just as my phone rings. I fish it out of my pocket and look at the incoming call. It's an unknown number.

I stand up, but it feels like my heart is still on the couch.

Adrenaline rushes through me as I swipe to answer the phone. It might be a telemarketer, but it might not be, so I rush across the living room and go outside to take the call in private.

"Hello?" No one says anything, so I repeat myself. "Hello? It's Daniel. Hello?"

If it is a telemarketer, they've probably never heard a guy sound so desperate to talk to one of them before.

A man clears his throat, and then says, "Hi. Daniel Wesley?"

I'm pacing the front yard, gripping the back of my neck. "Yes. Who is this?"

"I'm . . . well, I'm your child's father."

I stop pacing. In fact, I bend over at the waist when I hear those words. I feel like my stomach just fell onto the ground. I feel like *I'm* about to fall to the ground.

Holy. Fucking. Shit. Don't say anything stupid, Daniel. Don't screw this up.

"Do you have a second to chat?" the guy asks.

I nod frantically. "Yes. Yes, of course." I walk to the front patio and take a seat. I can barely feel my legs. "Thank you for calling, sir. Thank you so much. Can I just ask how he's doing? Is he good? Healthy? Is he happy?"

I should probably get Six for this conversation. I feel awful being feet away from her and she has no idea that I'm on the phone with a man who knows where our son is. But I'm worried there's a chance he's not calling with good news, so I stay seated until I can find out more information.

"He's . . ." The man is hesitant. He pauses for a moment. "Listen, Daniel. I don't know you. And I don't know my son's biological mother. But I know my wife, and she has been through hell. The last thing I want to do is bring stress or pain back into her life, because she's in such a good place right now. I need to know what your intentions are before I tell her you've reached out. Before I decide to share anything with you. I hope you understand that."

"She doesn't know you're talking to me right now?"

"No. She doesn't. And I haven't decided if I'm even going to tell her about this conversation yet."

Yet.

I cling to that word. That word means this phone call is the one deciding factor in whether or not Six and I will know what happened to our child.

Yeah, no pressure or anything. *Christ.*

I think about what Hannah said. *Be persistent.*

"Okay. Well. My name is Daniel. I'm nineteen. My girlfriend, Six . . . she's the biological mother. And . . ." I stand up again, feeling the pressure of this entire conversation and just how much is riding on my shoulders right now. "Sorry. I just need a minute."

The man says, "It's okay. Take all the time you need."

I blow out a calming breath. I look at the house and into the window of the kitchen. Six is in there, oblivious to what's going on out here. Oblivious to the fact that I'm speaking to a man who knows where her child is.

Our child.

But honestly . . . her child. The baby she grew and carried for nine months. The burden she still carries.

I know he's my son, but I'd be lying to myself if I said I was talking to this man and feeling this nervous because of how I feel about a child I've never met. I'm not doing this for him. I'm confident Six made the right choice.

Everything I'm doing, I'm doing for Six. And I don't want to let her down. She needs this more than anyone has ever needed anything. And sadly, the future of her happiness is in my hands. My tiny, tiny hands.

I blow out a calming breath, hoping I can be as candid as I need to be with this guy.

"Can I ask you a question?" I ask him.

"Go ahead."

"Why did you adopt him? Can you and your wife not have children?"

The man is silent for a moment. "No. We can't. We tried for several years, and then my wife had a hysterectomy."

I can hear in his voice how hard it was just for him to say that, much less live through it. It makes me think his wife has been through the same kind of pain Six has been through. "Would you have stayed married to her no matter what? If you adopted a baby or not?"

"Of course," the man says. "She's the love of my life. But this child means the world to us, so if you're thinking about trying to—"

"Just hear me out," I say. "Six is the love of *my* life. I

know I'm only nineteen, but she's the best thing that's ever happened to me. And seeing her sad is just . . . it's unbearable, man. It's fucking unbearable. She just needs to know he's okay. She needs to know she made the right decision. And I'd be lying to you if I said I need this, too, because I don't. Not as much as she does. I just want her to be whole again. This broke her. And until she knows her little boy is happy and healthy I don't know that she'll ever heal. So yeah, I guess that's all I'm asking for. I want to see her happy, and right now, you and your wife are literally the only people in the world who can give her that."

I press my hand to my forehead. I shouldn't have cussed. I said *fucking* and that probably annoyed him. I feel every bit of the immature teenager that I still am while talking to this man.

There's a long silence, but I know he's still on the phone because I hear him sigh heavily. Then he says, "I'll talk to my wife. I'm going to let this be her decision and I'm going to support whatever that decision is. I have your contact information. If you don't hear from us, I need to ask you to let this go. As much as I wish I could help you, I can't promise anything."

I pump my fist in the air. I try not to sound too excited when I say, "Okay. Thank you. That's all I was hoping for. Thank you."

"Daniel?" he says.

"Yes, sir?"

"However this turns out . . . *thank you.*"

He hasn't said a single word about our son, but I hear it all in that *thank you*. It has to mean our little boy is doing well and making them happy.

He hangs up after saying that.

And then I'm left with this emptiness. My God, it's so heavy.

Being so close but still so fucking far away.

I take a seat on the patio chair again. Part of me wants to run inside and swing Six around and tell her everything that just happened. Every word of that conversation. But the realistic side of me knows that the conversation I just had might mean absolutely nothing. I may never hear from him again. And if I don't, that means no matter how much I reach out to whoever I can reach out to, this couple's decision is final. And we're legally bound to accept that.

All our hope has been placed on this one conversation. This one woman.

We're in the middle of the biggest trial of our lives and we have a jury of one deciding our future.

"Hey."

I wipe my eyes and look away from the front door Six just walked out of. I stand up, with my back to her. I shove my phone into my pocket.

"Daniel? Are you crying?"

I run my hands under my eyes again. "No. Allergies." I turn and face her, plastering on the fakest smile I've ever given anyone.

"You don't have allergies."

"I don't?"

"No." She steps closer to me and puts her hands on my chest. Her eyes are filled with concern. "What's wrong? Why are you crying? You never cry."

I take her face in my hands and press my forehead to hers. I feel her arms snake around my waist. "Six, I tell you everything," I whisper. "But I don't want to talk about this. Not yet. Just give me time to process it, okay?"

"You're scaring me."

"I'm fine. Perfectly fine. I just had a moment and I need you to trust me." I wrap my arms around her and hug her tight. "I'm hungry. I just want to eat all the food and hang out with you and my friends and not think about anything else today. I'm fine. I promise."

She nods against my shoulder. "Okay. But I ruined the dressing, so pizza is on the way."

I laugh. "I figured as much."

Chapter Five

It's been eight hours since the man called. I've checked my phone every five minutes for an email or a missed call or a text.

Nothing.

He didn't say when he was going to talk to his wife. He might be waiting for the perfect moment. That could be weeks or months. Or maybe he already talked to her and she decided she didn't want communication.

Maybe I'm going to spend the rest of my life looking down at my phone, waiting for them to contact me. I should have told him to at least tell me if they chose not to communicate with us. At least then I would have a definitive answer.

"Your turn, Daniel," Jack says to me.

I rest my phone back on the table and roll the dice. I suggested we all play Monopoly when Jack and Karen got home earlier. I needed my mind to be on something else, but this game is so damn slow. Holder demands to be the banker because he doesn't trust me, and he counts everyone's money three times.

I move my thimble and land on Park Place. "I'll buy it," I say.

"That'll be three hundred and fifty dollars," Holder says.

I pay him in fives because, for some reason, it's all I have. I watch him count it. Then he counts it again. He starts to put it in the tray, but then he picks up the wad of fives and starts to count for a *third* time.

"*Christ*. Hurry the hell up," I groan.

"Language," Jack says.

"Sorry," I mutter.

Holder stops counting the money. He's just staring at me from across the table.

"You okay?" Six asks, concerned.

"I'm fine," I reassure her. "This game is just taking forever because Holder counts money like a blind mole."

"Bite me," Holder says as he resumes counting my money for the *third* time.

"Moles are actually blind, so saying *blind mole* is redundant," Breckin says.

I turn my head and glare at him. "Shut up, Powder Puff."

"Okay," Holder snaps, grabbing the Park Place card back from me. "You're done. Go home."

I snatch the card back from him. "No, we aren't finished. We're finishing this damn game."

"You're making this not fun," Sky says.

"Seriously," Six says. She squeezes my leg under the
table, a little forcefully. "Let's take a break. We can go to
my house and make out. That might make you feel better."

That actually sounds way better and a lot more distracting than this stupid game. I toss my Park Place card on the
center of the Monopoly board. "Good idea."

"Good riddance," Holder mutters.

I ignore them and walk toward the front door. Six apol-
ogizes on my behalf and that makes me feel like shit, but I
don't stop her. I'll apologize to everyone tomorrow.

I've just never felt this pent-up before. That phone call
left me wondering if this is how Six has felt this whole time.
Maybe she's felt this way since the day she put him up for
adoption, and if so, I'm a complete asshole for never rec-
ognizing it or trying to do something about it before this
week.

We've walked around to the side of her house because
she still uses her bedroom window whenever she returns
home from Sky's. Right before she pushes it open, I pull her
to me by her waist.

"I'm sorry. I love you."

"I love you, too," she says.

"I'm sorry I'm in a bad mood."

"It's okay. You were definitely a dick in there just now,
but I know you. You'll make it right."

"I will."

"I know," she says.

"I love you. No matter what."

"I know." She pushes open the window and says, "Come on, I'll let you touch my boobs. Maybe that'll get your mind off things."

"Both of them?"

"Sure." She climbs through the window and I follow her, wondering how I ended up with the only girl in the world who gets me.

And, despite knowing exactly who I am, she somehow still loves me.

When we're standing next to her bed, I kiss her and it's a good kiss. A distracting kiss. Right when I'm about to lower her to her bed, my phone vibrates in my pocket.

My adrenaline begins pumping even harder. I immediately pull away from her and look at the incoming text. I practically deflate when I see it's just a text from Holder.

You okay, man? Need to talk?

"It's just Holder," I say, as if Six was even wondering who texted me. I slide my phone back into my pocket.

Six sits on the bed and pulls me on top of her, and even though I've been a complete asshole tonight, she lets me make out with her for fifteen minutes straight. She even lets me take off her bra. We haven't had sex since the day in the maintenance closet, and that's been a long damn time.

But I like that we still have that to look forward to, and even though I can't wait for it to happen, tonight is not the night I want it to happen. I've been a brat tonight. She deserves to have sex with me when I'm not acting like a brat.

My phone vibrates again, but I ignore it this time. Holder can wait.

"I think you got another text," Six whispers.

"I know. It can wait."

Six pushes against my chest. "I have to pee, anyway."

I roll onto my back and watch her walk into the bathroom. I pull my phone out of my pocket and see a notification from my Gmail.

My heart twists into a knot and I hit the notification so hard I'm surprised I don't drop my phone.

It's an email from someone named Quinn Wells.

I don't know that name.

I don't know that name and that's good. This could be good. I'm standing now. Pacing. The toilet is flushing. I read the subject line.

Hi.

That's it. It just says *Hi*. I don't even know how to interpret that, so I keep reading.

Dear Six and Daniel,
      Graham told me about your conversation. It's odd, because I've written countless letters to the

biological mother of my child before, letters I knew I
would never send, but now that I know you'll actually
read this, I don't even know how to start.

"Oh my God, holy shit, fuck, fuck, *fuck yes!*" I cover my
mouth with my hand and stop reading because this isn't
something I should be reading alone. Six needs to read this,
too. She walks out of the bathroom and sees me standing by
her bed. I motion for her to hurry up and sit down.

"What?"

"Sit. Sit." I pat the bed and sit next to her and she's so
confused, but I can't find my words right now to explain
what's happening, so I just start rambling and hope she can
decipher it all. "So, I made some phone calls the other day.
And then this guy called me today and I didn't know if we
would hear anything back, so I didn't say anything to you,
but . . ."

I shove my phone into her hands. "Look. Look at this. I
haven't read it yet, but . . ."

Six grabs my phone, eyeing me with warranted concern.
She breaks our stare and looks at the phone screen. "Dear
Six and Daniel," she says aloud. "Graham told me about
your conversation. It's odd, because I've written countless
letters to the biological mother of my child before, letters I
knew . . ."

Six stops reading and looks up at me. I can see in her
eyes she has no idea what this is, and that she's hoping it's
what she thinks it is, but she's too scared to think that.

"It's them," I say, pointing down at my phone. "Quinn Wells. That's her name. And her husband's name must be Graham. Quinn and Graham. They have our baby."

Six drops the phone and covers her mouth. I've never seen eyes fill with tears as fast as hers just did. "Daniel?" she whispers. Her voice is cautious. She's scared to believe this.

I pick up the phone. "It's them," I say again.

"How?" She's shaking her head in complete disbelief. "I don't understand. You talked to her husband? But . . . *how?*"

She's too scared to read the email. I probably should have explained it all earlier so this moment wouldn't be so chaotic, but I didn't know he'd talk to her today and that she'd actually reach out, and *holy shit, I can't believe this is happening.*

"I called that teacher you mentioned. Ava. Hannah said I was annoying and that I needed to be persistent, and so I was and I literally begged her, Six. I didn't know if it would work, but then he called today and said he was going to leave the decision up to his wife. I'm sorry I didn't tell you, but I didn't want to get your hopes up because I wasn't sure if she would ever reach out. But she did."

Six's whole body is shaking from the sobs. She's crying so hard now. Way too hard to read an email. I pull her to me. "It's okay, babe. It's okay. This is good."

"How do you know?" she says through her tears. "What if she's emailing to tell us to leave them alone?"

She's terrified, but she doesn't need to be. I don't know how I know, because I haven't read the email yet, but something about her reaching out tells me it's good. Quinn's husband seemed to really hear me out today, and I just don't believe they would email us if it wasn't good.

"You want me to read it out loud?"

Six nods, tucking herself against me. I wrap my arm around her as she presses her face against my chest like she doesn't want to see the email. I pick up my phone and begin to read the letter out loud. I start from the very beginning again.

Dear Six and Daniel,

Graham told me about your conversation. It's odd, because I've written countless letters to the biological mother of my child before, letters I knew I would never send, but now that I know you'll actually read this, I don't even know how to start.

First, I want to take this opportunity to introduce myself. My name is Quinn Wells and my husband's name is Graham. We were both born and raised in Connecticut. Circumstances led us to Italy for a time, however, where we were fortunate enough to be given the gift of adopting your beautiful baby boy.

I have to put my phone down and take a breath. Six lifts her face from my chest and looks up at me, alarmed by my pause. I smile at her and wipe a tear away. "She said he's beautiful."

Six smiles.

"I don't think I can read this out loud," I say. "Let's read it together."

Both of us are complete wrecks now, so I reach over and grab some tissues from her bedside table and hand some to her. She sits up straighter and I hold up the phone. We lean our heads together and continue reading the email.

Our struggle with infertility has been a long one. It was very difficult for us to conceive, and when we finally did, it resulted in an unviable pregnancy and a hysterectomy. I don't want to inundate you with all the painful details, but please know that because of the struggles Graham and I have been through, our marriage has turned out stronger and full of more love than I could ever imagine.

And now, thanks to you, it is nothing short of perfect.

Being the young expectant mother you were, Six, I can't possibly imagine how difficult it must have been for you to make the decision to put your child up for adoption. Because I am unable to comprehend the pain you must have faced, I sometimes wonder if you are unable to comprehend our absolute elation and gratefulness to you.

My sister was the one who told us about you. You know her. Ava. She grew to love and respect you not only as one of her favorite students, but as a person.

Forgive me if I have any of the details wrong, as not a lot of information was disclosed about your situation. We were told that you were an American student in Italy on a foreign exchange. Ava informed us that you were looking for a family to adopt your child. We didn't want to get our hopes up because Graham and I have been let down many times in the past, but we wanted this more than anything.

The night Ava came to discuss the opportunity with us, I immediately told her to stop speaking. I didn't want to hear it. I was scared to death that it would be a situation that might not work out in the end. The thought of it not working out after getting my hopes up was more terrifying to me than never entertaining the idea of it.

After Ava left that night, Graham spoke to me about my fears. I will never forget the words he said that made me change my mind and open up my heart to the possibility. He said, "If you weren't completely terrified right now, I would be convinced that we aren't the right parents for this child, because becoming a parent should be the most terrifying thing to ever happen to a person."

As soon as he said that I knew he was absolutely right. Becoming a mother isn't about securing your own happiness. It's about taking the chance of being terrified and even devastated for the sake of a child.

That also applies to you, Six, as his biological

mother. I know it was a hard decision for you. But for whatever reason, you accepted a future of unknown fear in return for your child's happiness and security. I will never be able to thank you enough for that.

I'm still not sure why you chose us. Maybe it's because Ava was able to vouch for us or maybe it's because they told you our story. Or maybe it was chance. Whatever your reasons, I can assure you there are no two people in this world who could love your little boy more than Graham and I do.

We were advised by the lawyer to make it a closed adoption for various reasons. The main one being that it was supposed to give us peace of mind knowing that if you changed your mind and wanted to locate your child in the future, we would be protected.

However, the fact that you were unable to reach out to us because of the closed nature of the adoption has brought me very little peace of mind. I have been full of fear. Not an irrational fear of losing our son to you, but a substantial fear that you might go a lifetime not knowing this beautiful human you brought into the world.

Even though he's not quite a year old yet, he is the most incredible child. Sometimes, when I hold him, I wonder so many things. I wonder where he got the adorable heart shape of his mouth. I wonder if the head full of brown hair came from his mother or his father. I wonder if his playful personality is a reflection of the people who created him. There are so many wonderful things about him, and we want nothing more than to share those wonderful things with the people who blessed us with him.

We decided to name him Matteo Aaron Wells. We chose the name Aaron because it means "miraculous," and we chose Matteo because it's an Italian name meaning "gift." And that is exactly what Matteo is to us. A miraculous gift.

Graham and I made the decision to at least entertain the idea of reaching out to you a few weeks ago. We contacted our lawyer and requested your information, but I hadn't reached out yet because I was hesitant. Even this morning, after Graham told me about the phone call, I was still hesitant.

But then something happened about an hour ago. Matteo was in his high chair and Graham was feeding him mashed potatoes, and as soon as Matteo saw me when I walked into the room, he lifted his hands and said, "Mama."

It wasn't his first word, and it wasn't even the first time he said Mama, but it was the first time he applied the term specifically to me. I didn't know how hard it would hit me. How much it would mean to me. I immediately picked him up and pulled him to my chest and cried. Then Graham pulled me to his chest, and we stood there and cried together for several minutes. It was a ridiculous moment and maybe we were both way too excited about it, but it wasn't until this moment that it felt so real and permanent.

We're a family.

He's our son and we're his parents and none of this would have been possible without you.

As soon as Graham released me, I told him I needed to write this email. I want Matteo to know that not only does he have a mother and father in me and Graham, but he has an extra mother and father who care for him as deeply as we do. A biological mother who cares enough for him that she sacrificed her own happiness to see him have a life that she, for whatever reasons, felt she was unable to give him at the time of his birth.

We would love for you to meet him someday. Feel free to call us at the number below, or email us if you'd prefer. We would be honored to finally have the opportunity to thank you in person.

I've attached some photos of him. He's the happiest little boy I know, and I can't wait for him to become a significant part of both of your lives.

Thank you for our miraculous gift.

Sincerely,

Quinn, Graham, and Matteo Wells

We hug.

We hug and we cry. So hard.

Chapter Six

I don't even know how to describe this moment Six and I are sharing. It's the best thing that's ever happened to me. I don't know that I've ever cried tears of happiness. I don't know that I've ever seen Six cry so hard while laughing. We're just a big, stupid mess and it feels really, really phenomenal.

Every time I start to speak, we cry. Every time she starts to speak, we cry. We can't even talk and it's been five minutes since we finished the email.

We keep waiting for the attachments to load on my phone, but they're taking forever, so Six grabs her laptop. I log in to my email and hit download.

When the first picture loads, there isn't even enough air in the room to fill our collective gasps.

He looks just like me.

But he also looks just like her.

It's so weird and amazing, seeing this life we created, and it somehow makes me feel even closer to her.

"Oh my God," she whispers. "He's perfect."

"Scroll down," I say, too impatient to wait for more of him now that we got this small glimpse of him. We linger over each picture. We zoom in on his features. He has Six's mouth and my eyes and a headful of brown hair.

We even zoom in on his surroundings. It looks like he has a big backyard. A whole playset he's still too little to use. There are five pictures total, and after we look at them each twenty times, I say, "We should call them."

Six nods. "Yes." She clenches her stomach. "I'm so nervous."

"Me too. Me too, babe."

She sits on the edge of her bed and I stand and pace while I dial the number Quinn listed in the email. I put it on speaker, and when it starts ringing I sit down next to Six.

"This is Graham."

"Hi. Hey, it's me. Daniel. We just got your email." I feel like I should say more. Like *thank you* or *we love you* or *can we come meet him tonight?*

"Great," Graham says. "Let me grab Quinn."

The line goes quiet and Six and I look at each other nervously. Then a woman says, "Hi. This is Quinn. Is this Six and Daniel?"

"Yes," we both say at once.

"Thank you," Six blurts out. She's crying, but also smiling bigger than I've ever seen her smile. "Thank you so much. He's so perfect. We're so happy to see him so happy. Thank you." She covers her own mouth so she'll stop talking.

Quinn laughs. "Thank *you*," she says softly. "I meant every word."

"Where do you guys live?" I ask. "Are you still in Italy?"

"Oh. No, I forgot to mention that in the email. We moved back to Connecticut a few months ago. We wanted to be closer to Graham's parents."

"So, Matteo is here? In the same country?" I ask.

"Yep."

Six wipes at her eyes. "And you really don't mind if we meet him?"

"We would love that. But we know very little about either of you. Could you tell us a little about yourselves first? Where do you live?"

"We both go to college in Dallas," I say. "Six wants to be a psychologist."

"Psychiatrist," Six corrects him between tears.

"Something that ends in *ist*," I say. "I don't know what I want to be yet. We're both freshmen, so we're figuring things out as we go."

"And you're a couple? Still?"

"Yes. Well, we weren't technically a couple until after the baby was adopted. But we are now."

"I love that," Quinn says.

"Daniel is the best," Six says. "You'll love him." She looks at me and smiles. I squeeze her hand.

"You'll love Six more."

"I already love you both because of what you've given us," Quinn says. "Well, we know you guys are dying to meet him, but we don't want you to miss too much college. We would say come next weekend, but we'd like you to be able to stay more than just a day or two. How does Christmas break sound? It's just a few weeks away."

That sounds like a lifetime.

I can see Six feels the same way because she deflates a little. But then she says, "That's perfect. We'll be there."

"Yes. We'll be there," I confirm.

Quinn says, "Do you need help with the cost of flights?"

"No, you guys have done enough," Six says. "Truly."

There's a pause, and then Graham takes over the phone. "We have each other's numbers now. We'll text you our address. Just let us know what days you want to come and we'll work our schedules around it. We're looking forward to it."

"Thank you," Six says again.

"Yes. Thank you," I add.

Six is squeezing my hand so hard, it kind of hurts. Graham and Quinn both say goodbye. When I hang up the phone, we sit in silence for a moment, letting it all sink in.

"Shit," I mutter.

"What?"

I look at Six. "This means we have to tell our parents that they're grandparents."

Six looks worried, but only for a second. Then she grins. "My brothers are going to hate you."

I would expect that to alarm me, but it doesn't. "I don't care. Nothing can bring me down from this high."

Six laughs and then stands up, pulling my hands. "We have to go tell Sky and Holder!" Six crawls out her window and then through Sky's bedroom window. I'm right on her heels.

When we burst into the living room from the hallway, everyone looks up at us. They're still playing Monopoly.

"We found him!" Six says.

I'm sure they can all tell we've been crying, which would explain why they seem so alarmed by the sight of us.

"Found who?" Karen asks.

Sky immediately knows what we're talking about and why we look so disheveled and elated. She stands up slowly and covers her mouth. Then she says, "No."

Six nods. "Yes. We just got off the phone with them. We get to meet him next month."

"Meet who?" Breckin says.

"The baby?" Holder says.

I nod. "Yes. His name is Matteo. And he's adorable. He looks just like us."

"Who is Matteo?" Karen asks.

"What is everyone talking about?" Jack asks.

Holder and Sky are rushing across the room. Holder must not even care that I lost my cool with him earlier because he pulls me in for a hug. Six and Sky are hugging and squealing. Then all four of us are hugging. *God, I've done a lot of hugging this week.*

When we all let go, Jack and Karen and Breckin are still staring at us. More than annoyed. "What's going on?" Karen asks Sky.

Sky answers for us. "Daniel got Six pregnant and she had the baby in Italy and put it up for adoption and they found him!"

"I didn't know I got her pregnant," I say. I don't know why I say that.

"I didn't know it was Daniel who got me pregnant," Six says.

"It's complicated," Holder adds.

Karen's eyes are wide. She's staring at Six. "You . . . you had a *baby?*"

Six nods. "Yeah, and no offense, but we don't have time to explain right now. We've got to go tell our parents that they're grandparents now."

"Your parents don't know?" Jack says. For some reason, he looks at Holder and glares at him. "Anything you and Sky want to share with us now that this is all out in the open?"

Holder shakes his head. "No. No, sir. No babies here. Not yet. I mean, not for a long time. Years."

As much as I like seeing Holder nervous, Six and I have stuff to do. People to inform. Parents to piss off. I grab her hand and lead her to the front door. "Sorry I was a dick earlier!" I yell back to everyone. Then I look at Breckin. "I'll never call you Powder Puff again. I'm a dad now, I have to set a good example."

Breckin nods. "Thanks. I think."

Six pushes me out the door. "Let's tell your parents first," she says. "We'll tell mine in the morning. They're already in bed."

Chapter Seven

Six and I are seated on the love seat together. She's clutching my hand. Hannah and Chunk are on the couch. My parents are too worried to sit down, so they're pacing the living room.

"You're scaring us, Daniel," my mother says.

"What is this about?" my father asks me. "You never call Wesley family meetings." He looks at Six. "Oh my God. Are you pregnant? Did Daniel get you pregnant?"

We glance at each other and then Six says, "No. Well . . . not . . . technically."

"You want to *get* pregnant?" he asks, still throwing out guesses.

"No," Six says.

"You're engaged?" my mother asks me.

"No," I say.

"Sick?" she asks.

I wish they'd just shut up and let me form my thoughts. This is a tough thing to blurt out.

"You're breaking up?" my father asks.

"You dropped out of college?" my mother asks.

"For Pete's sake, they had a baby!" Chunk yells, annoyed. Then she immediately slaps her hand over her mouth and looks at me with eyes as wide as saucers. "Sorry, Daniel. I was getting really irritated with all the guessing."

"It's fine," I assure her.

My parents look at me in dumbfounded silence. And confusion. "You . . . *what?*"

"Six and I . . . we um . . ." I struggle to find my words.

"We had sex in a dark closet about a year before we formally met," Six says. "I got pregnant. Found out on a foreign exchange in Italy. I didn't know who I had sex with, which meant I didn't know who the father was, so I gave the baby up for adoption. But when I moved back and started dating Daniel, we figured it out. And now we know where our baby is and we're going to meet him over Christmas break."

That wasn't as delicate as I was hoping it would be, but it's out there now.

And my parents are still silent.

"Sorry," I mutter. "We used a condom."

I expect them to be angry or sad, but instead, my father begins to laugh.

So does my mother.

"Good one," my father says. "But we aren't falling for it."

"It's not a prank," I say.

I look to Hannah and Chunk for backup, but their jaws are practically dragging the floor. "Wait," Hannah says. "You found him? You actually *found* him?"

Oh yeah. I forgot Hannah and Chunk didn't know that part.

Six nods and pulls out her phone to show Hannah. "They emailed us tonight."

Hannah grabs the phone from Six.

My mother looks at Chunk like she's the only one who will be honest with her. "It's true," Chunk says. "Daniel told us a couple days ago. It really happened."

"We have pictures," I say, pulling out my phone.

My mother shakes her head and starts pacing again. "Daniel, if this is a joke, I will never forgive you."

"It isn't a joke, Mrs. Wesley," Six says. "I would never joke about something like this."

"Look, I know it's a shock."

My father holds his hand up to shut me up. "You had a baby and put him up for adoption and didn't tell us?"

"He didn't know until after it happened," Six says in my defense. "I didn't know who the father was."

My father is standing next to my mother, still glaring down at me. "How could you not—"

My mother puts a hand on my father's shoulder so he won't finish that sentence. "We need a minute," my mother says to us.

Six and I look at each other. We've been so excited I

don't think we really thought about how this would go down with our parents. We go to my bedroom, but we wait with the door slightly open so we can listen to what they have to say. But nothing is said. Just sighs. Lots of sighs.

My father is the first to speak. "Do we ground him?" he asks my mother.

"He's nineteen."

Another pause. Then, "We're *grand*parents?" my mother says.

"We aren't old enough to be grandparents."

"Obviously, we are. And they said it was a boy?" she asks.

"Yeah. A boy. Our boy had a boy. Our son has a son. *My* son has his own son. I have a grandson."

"So do I," my mother mutters disbelievingly.

Six and I just wait patiently and listen as they work it out.

"I'm not ready to be a grandmother," my mother says.

"Well, you are."

"I wonder what his name is?" she asks my father.

I take it upon myself to answer this one. "Matteo!" I yell down the hallway as I poke my head out of the bedroom.

My father peeks down the hallway from the living room. When I see him, I open my door all the way. We stare at each other for a moment. He looks disappointed. I'd almost rather him look angry. "Well," he says, motioning for us to come back to the living room, "let's see the pictures."

We take a seat at our dining room table and my parents

and my sisters pass my phone around, taking turns looking at the pictures. It takes a good ten minutes to sink in before my mother starts crying. "He's so beautiful," she says.

Six is squeezing my hand again. Then she starts to cry, because when Six sees anyone else cry, it makes *her* cry. "I'm sorry I let someone adopt him," she says to my parents. "I didn't know what else to do."

My mother's eyes swing to Six and she's immediately out of her chair. She takes Six's hands and locks eyes with her. "You have nothing to apologize for. Nothing at all. We love you so much, Six."

They hug, and dammit if it doesn't make *me* tear up. As much as they embarrass me, I really did get lucky when it comes to parents.

Hell. I might have even gotten lucky when it comes to sisters, too.

"I want to meet him," Chunk says. "When can we meet him?"

"Hopefully you all will. But we think it should just be the two of us this first trip."

Everyone seems to be in agreement with that.

"Oh, and one more thing," I add, turning to my parents. "Could you buy us plane tickets to Connecticut?"

Chapter Eight

Three weeks later

We agreed to take an Uber to their house from the airport. Meeting our child for the first time in an airport seemed too stale.

We don't speak much on the way there. It's been the longest three weeks of both of our lives, and as much as we wanted to call them every day, we held off. We didn't want to scare them away.

"Neighborhood seems nice," I say as we grow closer. All the houses are decorated for Christmas. I look over at Six and she looks so nervous. Her skin is pale.

When we pull up to the address, we stare out the window for a moment. It's a nice house. Bigger than anything Six and I would be raising him in. Not that the size of the house matters, but I can't help but want the very best for him.

"You ready?" I ask Six.

She shakes her head. Her eyes are red, and I can tell she's trying not to cry.

This is a huge moment for us. It's terrifying. But our Uber driver doesn't get that because he says, "Hey, I don't get paid for you guys to sit in my back seat and cry."

That irritates the hell out of me. I bump the back of his headrest. "She's about to meet her child for the first time, Dick Prick! Give us a minute! Also, it smells like tacos in here. Get an air freshener."

The Uber driver meets my glare in the rearview mirror and then mutters, "Sorry. Take your time. Didn't know this was a big moment."

"Well, it is," I mutter.

Six rolls her eyes at me. "It's fine," she says, sniffling. "I'm ready. Let's do this."

We get out of the car and I go around to the trunk to grab our suitcases. One of them is filled with a week's worth of our clothes. The other one is filled with toys and clothes from everyone: Sky and Holder, Karen and Jack, Breckin, both sets of our parents. Even Six's brothers, who really did give me a hard time after they found out, pitched in a few presents before we left.

The Uber driver actually makes himself useful and helps me with one of the suitcases. When he shuts the trunk, he looks at me. "Does it really smell like tacos in my car?"

I shrug. "Yeah. But the good kind."

"I had tacos for lunch. You have a good nose."

I kind of feel bad for snapping at the guy now, but he shouldn't rush his passengers like that. "I wasn't trying to insult you. I love tacos."

The driver shrugs it off. "It's cool. And hey, I'm also an Uber Eats driver. I can actually go get you tacos if you want some. There's this really great taco stand over on Jackson Street."

I *am* hungry. "How good? I'm from Texas and we have really good tacos in Texas."

"Dude, they're the best tacos you'll ever—"

"Daniel?" Six interrupts our conversation. She lifts a hand and waves it at the house behind her. "We're about to meet our son in a matter of seconds and you're seriously going to sit here and make me wait while you have a full-on conversation about *tacos*?"

"I . . . Sorry. I just love tacos."

"Tacos are great," the driver mutters. "Good luck with your kid and stuff." He gets back in the car and cranks it. We look up at the house just as the front door opens. A man walks out. I guess this is Graham.

"Shit," I whisper. "He's good-looking. I don't know why that makes me even more nervous."

"His socks don't match," Six says as we make our way up the driveway. "I like him already."

We meet Graham at the front door. He shakes my hand and introduces himself. "You must be Daniel," he says. He looks at Six and hugs her. "And Six." He pulls back and opens the front door. "How was your flight?"

We follow him inside and I set the two suitcases by their front door. "It was good," I say, looking around. This is so weird. Being here. I feel like I'm about to puke. I can't imagine how Six feels right now.

There are pictures lining the hallway that leads to the living room. Six and I walk slowly and look at them. Most we've seen, but some we haven't.

Quinn appears around the corner and she's exactly how I assumed she would be. Welcoming and happy and full of just as many emotions as Six. She introduces herself and then we're all just kind of awkwardly standing around.

"Are you ready to meet Matteo?" Quinn asks.

Six blows out a breath, shaking out her hands. "I don't want to scare him. I have to collect myself."

"Don't worry about that," Graham says. "We've spent the first year of his life emotional wrecks. Sometimes we just burst into tears while we're holding him because we're so damn lucky." Graham and Quinn smile at each other.

Graham motions for us to follow them into the living room, where we finally see our son. He's lying on the floor, surrounded by toys.

Seeing him in pictures was one thing but seeing him in person is an entirely different experience. Six squeezes my hand and we both gasp. I suddenly don't feel good enough to be here. Worthy enough.

And now all I can picture is Wayne and Garth, bowing down and chanting, *"We're not worthy. We're not worthy."* I kind of want to drop to my knees in front of this beautiful little boy and do the same thing.

Quinn picks up Matteo and walks him over to us.

We both start to cry. Six touches his arm with her fingers and then his hair. Then she pulls her hand back and covers her mouth.

"You want to hold him?" Quinn asks.

Six nods, so Quinn hands Matteo over to her. Six pulls him against her chest and presses her cheek against his head. She closes her eyes and just stands there, breathing him in.

It's fucking beautiful.

I want to take pictures, but that would be weird. I just never want to forget this. This whole damn moment. Seeing Six with our baby. Our happy and healthy and perfect baby. Seeing Six smiling. Seeing that piece of her that's been missing for so long finally reconnect all the broken parts of her.

We sit down on the couch with Matteo and take turns holding him.

"What's he like?" I ask. "Is he shy? Outgoing? Does he cry a lot? My mom said I was a crier."

"He's really friendly," Graham says. "Like he's never met a stranger."

Six laughs. "He gets that from Daniel."

Graham and Quinn are seated on the sofa opposite us. They don't look nervous at all about us being here. Quinn is snuggled against Graham, her hand on his chest. They're both smiling. It's almost as if a part of them was needing this, too.

"He's not a crier," Quinn says. "But he has a good set of lungs on him. Likes to hear himself jabber."

"He also gets that from me," I say.

We chat for a while, both of us continuing to take turns with Matteo. After we've been there for about an hour, Quinn is showing Six an album full of baby pictures.

Graham stands up and stretches out his arms, then drops his hands to his hips. He nudges his head toward the kitchen.

"Wanna help me with dinner, Daniel?"

I stand up, but I feel like I should warn him. "I can try, but I tend to only make the cooking experience worse."

Graham laughs, but heads into the kitchen anyway, expecting me to follow him. He takes vegetables out of the refrigerator and sets them on the counter. He slides a knife toward me and then rolls a tomato across the island. "Think you can cut a tomato?"

"First time for everything," I say. I start to cut the tomato while Graham assembles the rest of the salad. I feel like I should thank him, but I'm so awkward when it comes to having sincere conversations. I clear my throat. When he looks at me, I keep my eyes on the tomato I'm butchering. "I can't thank you enough for doing this for Six."

Graham says nothing. When I glance up at him, he's staring at me. He smiles a little and then says, "I didn't do it for Six. I did it for you."

That makes me pause.

"When I called you that day on the phone, I was honestly prepared to tell you to take a hike."

I release the knife and the tomato and then press my palms into the counter. "Really?"

Graham nods as he meticulously chops up an onion. "I had no interest in bringing potential stress into Quinn's life. I didn't think it would be good in any capacity to have Matteo's biological parents in the picture. I've seen the stories on the news, in the papers. The devastating custody battles. I didn't want to open that door. But when I called you . . . I don't know. I could hear the desperation in your voice. I could relate to the fact that all you wanted in that moment was to see the woman you loved happy." He makes eye contact with me across the island. "You reminded me of myself, and what that felt like. The agony that comes along with not being able to take the pain away from the person you love more than yourself."

Dammit. Maybe it's the onions. I don't know. I have to look away from him because I feel my eyes dampen. I grab my shirtsleeve and dab at them. "Those are some strong onions, man," I mutter.

Graham laughs. "Yeah. I guess so."

When I've composed myself, I go back to helping Graham with the salad. Quinn walks into the kitchen and looks at the tomato on my cutting board. She laughs.

"What have you done to that poor tomato?"

"I tried to warn Graham that I'm bad luck in a kitchen."

Quinn motions for the knife. "I'll take over. Go hang out in the living room with your family."

I smile at her and let her take over. But when I leave the kitchen, I have to pause to collect myself in the hallway.

She just called us a family.

"Fucking onions," I mutter to myself.

I walk back into the living room and sit down on the couch next to my girlfriend and our little boy. I spend the whole time watching them together as I try not to cry. But damn, my emotions are being tested more today than any other time in my life.

Today has honestly been filled with the best moments I've ever spent with Six. Better than the maintenance closet, better than our first date, better than all the days we've ever spent together combined. The last three agonizing weeks of waiting to be sitting here with our son have been torture.

But this?

This is perfection.

A damn Christmas miracle.

Chapter Nine

We'll be staying in their guest room for the week. At first, we were hesitant about it because we didn't want to impose. But they insisted, and we're two broke kids in college, so free sounded better than any other option. Apparently, Quinn's sister, Ava, spoke so highly of Six they felt like they knew her before they even invited us to meet Matteo. I'm sure it was hard for them, trusting us enough to not only bring us into their lives, but to also welcome us into their home.

I'm glad we chose to stay with the Wellses because we really like them. Graham seems like a stand-up guy. He laughs at my jokes. That's important to me. And Quinn and Six hit it off immediately.

After they put Matteo to sleep, we stayed up for two hours, the four of us, just talking and sharing our stories. They've been through a lot, but knowing the outcome and how happy they seem makes me think that Six and I can keep what we have forever. True love exists and the people in this house are proof of that.

"Matteo seems so happy," Six says, falling onto the bed.

"So do they," I say. "Did you see the way Graham looks at Quinn? Eleven years of marriage and he still looks at her like I look at you."

Six rolls onto her side and smiles at me. She rests a gentle hand on my cheek and brushes her thumb over my lips. "Thank you," she whispers. "You have no idea how much you've changed my life."

"Yeah?"

She nods. "Yeah. I know he's okay now. That's all I've ever wanted. And he's going to know us. We'll see him as often as we can. And I love them so much. *So* much. I was worried that meeting Matteo and the people who adopted him might make it worse. But when I see him with them, it's like he's theirs and I'm okay with that. He is theirs. He's ours *and* theirs." She leans forward. "I love you, Daniel Wesley," she whispers, her mouth brushing mine. "I finally feel connected again."

Six and I have kissed a lot since we've been together, but it's never felt quite like this. Now it's peaceful and good. Like we're both in the best place either of us has ever been.

I love her so much. Sometimes I love her so much it makes me feel like I might puke. Like there's so much love, it fills me up until I'm nauseated. In a good way. If nausea can ever be good.

Six rolls on top of me, and I don't know what's about to happen or how far this kiss will go. Maybe really far. Like all the way. Or maybe not far at all.

It doesn't even matter because today is perfect. Today is the best day of my life and it'll always be the best day of my life. No matter what.

Six pulls the covers over our heads. "I'm really proud of you," she says. "You went the whole night without cussing. And you didn't even give Matteo a nickname. I was sure you were going to slip up and call him Salty Balls or something."

That makes me laugh. "We'll be here for a week. There's plenty of time for me to slip up."

Six kisses my chin. Then my mouth. Then she kisses my . . .

Well. What happens next is no one's business but ours.

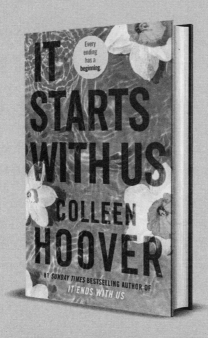
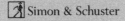

If you haven't read

ALL YOUR PERFECTS

read on to discover the
first chapter now...

Chapter One

Then

The doorman didn't smile at me.

That thought plagues me during the entire ride up the elevator to Ethan's floor. Vincent has been my favorite doorman since Ethan moved into this apartment building. He always smiles and chats with me. But today, he simply held the door open with a stoic expression. Not even a, *"Hello, Quinn. How was your trip?"*

We all have bad days, I guess.

I look down at my phone and see that it's already after seven. Ethan should be home at eight, so I'll have plenty of time to surprise him with dinner. *And myself*. I came back a day early but decided not to tell him. We've been doing so much planning for our wedding; it's been weeks since we had an actual home-cooked meal together. Or even sex.

When I reach Ethan's floor, I pause as soon as I step out

of the elevator. There's a guy pacing the hallway directly in front of Ethan's apartment. He takes three steps, then pauses and looks at the door. He takes another three steps in the other direction and pauses again. I watch him, hoping he'll leave, but he never does. He just keeps pacing back and forth, looking at Ethan's door. I don't think he's a friend of Ethan's. I would recognize him if he were.

I walk toward Ethan's apartment and clear my throat. The guy faces me and I motion toward Ethan's door to let him know I need to get past him. The guy steps aside and makes room for me but I'm careful not to make further eye contact with him. I fish around in my purse for the key. When I find it, he moves beside me, pressing a hand against the door. "Are you about to go in there?"

I glance up at him and then back at Ethan's door. *Why is he asking me that?* My heart begins to race at the thought of being alone in a hallway with a strange guy who's wondering if I'm about to open a door to an empty apartment. *Does he know Ethan isn't home? Does he know I'm alone?*

I clear my throat and try to hide my fear, even though the guy looks harmless. But I guess evil doesn't have a telling exterior, so it's hard to judge. "My fiancé lives here. He's inside," I lie.

The guy nods vigorously. "Yeah. He's inside all right." He clenches his fist and taps the wall next to the door. "Inside my fucking girlfriend."

I took a self-defense class once. The instructor taught us to slide a key between our fingers, poking outward, so if you're attacked you can stab the attacker in the eye. I do this, prepared for the psycho in front of me to lunge any second now.

He blows out a breath and I can't help but notice the air between us fills with the smell of cinnamon. What a strange thought to have in the moment before I'm attacked. What an odd lineup that would be at the police station. *"Oh, I can't really tell you what my attacker was wearing, but his breath smelled good. Like Big Red."*

"You have the wrong apartment," I tell him, hoping he'll walk away without an argument.

He shakes his head. Tiny little fast shakes that indicate I couldn't be more wrong and he couldn't be more right. "I have the right apartment. I'm positive. Does your fiancé drive a blue Volvo?"

Okay, so he's stalking Ethan? My mouth is dry. Water would be nice.

"Is he about six foot tall? Black hair, wears a North Face jacket that's too big for him?"

I press a hand against my stomach. *Vodka would be nice.*

"Does your fiancé work for Dr. Van Kemp?"

Now *I'm* the one shaking my head. Not only does Ethan work for Dr. Van Kemp . . . his father *is* Dr. Van Kemp. *How does this guy know so much about Ethan?*

"My girlfriend works with him," he says, glancing at the apartment door with disgust. "*More* than works with him, apparently."

"Ethan wouldn't . . ."

I'm interrupted by it. *The fucking.*

I hear Ethan's name being called out in a faint voice. At least it's faint from this side of the door. Ethan's bedroom is against the far side of his apartment, which indicates that whoever she is, she isn't being quiet about it. She's screaming his name.

While he fucks her.

I immediately back away from the door. The reality of what is happening inside Ethan's apartment makes me dizzy. It makes my whole world unstable. My past, my present, my future—all of it is spinning out of control. The guy grips my arm and stabilizes me. "You okay?" He steadies me against the wall. "I'm sorry. I shouldn't have blurted it out like that."

I open my mouth, but uncertainty is all that comes out. "Are you . . . are you sure? Maybe those sounds aren't coming from Ethan's apartment. Maybe it's the couple in the apartment next door."

"That's convenient. Ethan's neighbor is named Ethan, too?"

It's a sarcastic question, but I immediately see the regret in his eyes after he says it. That's nice of him—finding it in himself to feel compassion for me when he's obviously experiencing the same thing. "I followed them," he says. "They're in there together. My girlfriend and your . . . boyfriend."

"Fiancé," I correct.

I walk across the hallway and lean against the wall, then eventually slide down to the floor. I probably shouldn't plop myself on the floor because I'm wearing a skirt. Ethan likes skirts, so I thought I'd be nice and wear one for him, but now I want to take my skirt off and tie it around his neck and choke him with it. I stare at my shoes for so long, I don't even notice that the guy is sitting on the floor next to me until he says, "Is he expecting you?"

I shake my head. "I was here to surprise him. I've been out of town with my sister."

Another muffled scream makes its way through the door. The guy next to me cringes and covers his ears. I cover mine, too. We sit like this for a while. Both of us refusing to allow the noises to penetrate our ears until it's over. It won't last long. Ethan can't last more than a few minutes.

Two minutes later I say, "I think they're finished." The guy pulls his hands from his ears and rests his arms on his knees. I wrap my arms around mine, resting my chin on top of them. "Should we use my key to open the door? Confront them?"

"I can't," he says. "I need to calm down first."

He seems pretty calm. Most men I know would be breaking down the door right now.

I'm not even sure I want to confront Ethan. Part of me wants to walk away and pretend the last few minutes didn't happen. I could text him and tell him I came home early and he could tell me he's working late and I could remain blissfully ignorant.

Or I could just go home, burn all his things, sell my wedding dress, and block his number.

No, my mother would never allow that.

Oh, God. My mother.

I groan and the guy immediately sits up straight. "Are you about to be sick?"

I shake my head. "No. I don't know." I pull my head from my arms and lean back against the wall. "It just hit me how pissed my mother is going to be."

He relaxes when he sees I'm not groaning from physical illness, but rather from the dread of my mother's reaction when she finds out the wedding is off. Because it's definitely off. I lost count of how many times she's mentioned how much the deposit was in order to get on the waiting list at the venue. "Do you realize how many people wish they could get married at Douglas Whimberly Plaza? Evelyn Bradbury was married there, Quinn. *Evelyn Bradbury!*"

My mother loves to compare me to Evelyn Bradbury. Her family is one of the few in Greenwich who is more prominent than my stepfather's. So of course my mother uses Evelyn Bradbury as an example of high-class perfection at every opportunity. I don't care about Evelyn Bradbury. I have half a mind to text my mother right now and simply say, The wedding is off and I don't give a fuck about Evelyn Bradbury.

"What's your name?" the guy asks.

I look at him and realize it's the first time I've really taken him in. This might be one of the worst moments of his life, but even taking that into consideration, he's extremely handsome. Expressive dark brown eyes that match his unruly hair. A strong jaw that's been constantly twitching with silent rage since I walked out of the elevator. Two full lips that keep being pressed together and thinned out every time he glances at the door. It makes me wonder if his features would appear softer if his girlfriend weren't in there with Ethan right now.

There's a sadness about him. Not one related to our current situation. Something deeper . . . like it's embedded in him. I've met people who smile with their eyes, but he frowns with his.

"You're better looking than Ethan." My comment takes him off guard. His expression is swallowed up in confusion because he thinks I'm hitting on him. That's the last thing I'm doing right now. "That wasn't a compliment. It was just a realization."

He shrugs like he wouldn't care either way.

"It's just that if you're better looking than Ethan, that

makes me think your girlfriend is better looking than me. Not that I care. Maybe I do care. I *shouldn't* care, but I can't help but wonder if Ethan is more attracted to her than he is to me. I wonder if that's why he's cheating. Probably. I'm sorry. I'm usually not this self-deprecating but I'm so angry and for some reason I just can't stop talking."

He stares at me a moment, contemplating my odd train of thought. "Sasha is ugly. You have nothing to worry about."

"Sasha?" I say her name incredulously, then I repeat her name, putting emphasis on the *sha*. "Sa*sha*. That explains a lot."

He laughs and then *I* laugh and it's the strangest thing. Laughing when I should be crying. Why am I not crying?

"I'm Graham," he says, reaching out his hand.

"Quinn."

Even his smile is sad. It makes me wonder if his smile would be different under different circumstances.

"I would say it's good to meet you, Quinn, but this is the worst moment of my life."

That is a very miserable truth. "Same," I say, disappointed. "Although, I'm relieved I'm meeting you now rather than next month, after the wedding. At least I won't be wasting marriage vows on him now."

"You're supposed to get married next month?" Graham looks away. "What an asshole," he says quietly.

"He really is." I've known this about Ethan all along. He's an asshole. Pretentious. But he's good to me. *Or so I thought.* I lean forward again and run my hands through my hair. "God, this sucks."

As always, my mother has perfect timing with her incoming text. I retrieve my phone and look down at it.

Your cake tasting has been moved to two o'clock on Saturday. Don't eat lunch beforehand. Will Ethan be joining us?

I sigh with my whole body. I've been looking forward to the cake tasting more than any other part of the wedding planning. I wonder if I can avoid telling anyone the wedding is off until Sunday.

The elevator dings and my attention is swept away from my phone and to the doors. When they open, I feel a knot form in my throat. My hand clenches in a fist around my phone when I see the containers of food. The delivery guy begins to walk toward us and my heart takes a beating with every step. *Way to pour salt on my wounds, Ethan.*

"Chinese food? Are you kidding me?" I stand up and look down at Graham who is still on the floor, looking up at me. I wave my hand toward the Chinese food. "That's *my* thing! Not his! *I'm* the one who likes Chinese food after sex!" I turn back toward the delivery guy and he's frozen, staring at me, wondering if he should proceed to the door or not. "Give me that!" I take the bags from him. He doesn't even question me. I plop back down on the floor with the two bags of Chinese food and I rifle through them. I'm pissed to see that Ethan simply duplicated what I always order. "He even ordered the same thing! He's feeding Sasha my Chinese food!"

Graham jumps up and pulls his wallet out of his pocket. He pays for the food and the poor delivery guy pushes open the door to the stairwell just to get out of the hallway faster than if he were to walk back to the elevator.

"Smells good," Graham says. He sits back down and grabs the container of chicken and broccoli. I hand him a fork and let him eat it, even though the chicken is my favorite. This isn't a time to be selfish, though. I open the Mongolian beef and start eating, even though I'm not hungry. But I'll be damned if Sasha or Ethan will eat any of this. "Whores," I mutter.

"Whores with no food," Graham says. "Maybe they'll both starve to death."

I smile.

Then I eat and wonder how long I'm going to sit out here in the hallway with this guy. I don't want to be here when the door opens because I don't want to see what Sasha looks like. But I also don't want to miss the moment when she opens the door and finds Graham sitting out here, eating her Chinese food.

So I wait. And eat. With Graham.

After several minutes, he sets down his container and reaches into the takeout bag, pulling out two fortune cookies. He hands one to me and proceeds to open his. He breaks open the cookie and unfolds the strip of paper, then reads his fortune out loud. "You will succeed in a great business endeavor today." He folds the fortune in half after reading it. "Figures. I took off work today."

"Stupid fortune," I mutter.

Graham wads his fortune into a tiny ball and flicks it at Ethan's door. I crack open my cookie and slip the fortune out of it. "If you only shine light on your flaws, all your perfects will dim."

"I like it," he says.

I wad up the fortune and flick it at the door like he did. "I'm a grammar snob. It should be your *perfections*."

"That's what makes me like it. The one word they misuse is *perfects*. Kind of ironic." He crawls forward and grabs the fortune, then scoots back against the wall. He hands it to me. "I think you should keep it."

I immediately brush his hand and the fortune away. "I don't want a reminder of this moment."

He stares at me in thought. "Yeah. Me neither."

I think we're both growing more nervous at the prospect of the door opening any minute, so we just listen for their voices and don't speak. Graham pulls at the threads of his blue jeans over his right knee until there's a small pile of threads on the floor and barely anything covering his knee. I pick up one of the threads and twist it between my fingers.

"We used to play this word game on our laptops at night," he says. "I was really good at it. I'm the one who introduced Sasha to the game, but she would always beat my score. Every damn night." He stretches his legs out. They're a lot longer than mine. "It used to impress me until I saw an eight-hundred-dollar charge for the game on her bank statement. She was buying extra letters at five dollars a pop just so she could beat me."

I try to picture this guy playing games on his laptop at night, but it's hard. He looks like the kind of guy who reads novels and cleans his apartment twice a day and folds his socks and then tops off all that perfection with a morning run.

"Ethan doesn't know how to change a tire. We've had two flats since we've been together and he had to call a tow truck both times."

Graham shakes his head a little and says, "I'm not looking for reasons to excuse the bastard, but that's not so bad. A lot of guys don't know how to change a tire."

"I know. That's not the bad part. The bad part is that I *do* know how to change a tire. He just refused to let me because it would have embarrassed him to have to stand aside while a girl changed his tire."

There's something more in Graham's expression. Something I haven't noticed before. Concern, maybe? He pegs me with a serious stare. "Do *not* forgive him for this, Quinn."

His words make my chest tighten. "I won't," I say with complete confidence. "I don't want him back after this. I keep wondering why I'm not crying. Maybe that's a sign."

He has a knowing look in his eye, but then the lines around his eyes fall a little. "You'll cry tonight. In bed. That's when it'll hurt the most. When you're alone."

Everything suddenly feels heavier with that comment. I don't want to cry but I know this is all going to hit me any minute now. I met Ethan right after I started college and we've been together four years now. That's a lot to lose in one moment. And even though I know it's over, I don't want to confront him. I just want to walk away and be done with him. I don't want to need closure or even an explanation, but I'm scared I'll need both of those things when I'm alone tonight.

"We should probably get tested."

Graham's words and the fear that consumes me after he says them are cut off by the sound of Ethan's muffled voice.

He's walking toward the door. I turn to look at his apartment door but Graham touches my face and pulls my attention back to him.

"The worst thing we could do right now is show emotion, Quinn. Don't get angry. Don't cry."

I bite my lip and nod, trying to hold back all the things I know I'm about to need to scream. "Okay," I whisper, right as Ethan's apartment door begins to open.

I try to hold my resolve like Graham is doing, but Ethan's

looming presence makes me nauseous. Neither of us looks at the door. Graham's stare is hard and he's breathing steadily as he keeps his gaze locked on mine. I can't even imagine what Ethan will think in two seconds when he opens the door fully. He won't recognize me at first. He'll think we're two random people sitting on the hallway floor of his apartment building.

"Quinn?"

I close my eyes when I hear Ethan say my name. I don't turn toward his voice. I hear Ethan take a step out of his apartment. I can feel my heart in so many places right now, but mostly I feel it in Graham's hands on my cheeks. Ethan says my name again, but it's more of a command to look at him. I open my eyes, but I keep them focused on Graham.

Ethan's door opens even wider and a girl gasps in shock. *Sasha.* Graham blinks, holding his eyes closed for a second longer as he inhales a calming breath. When he opens them, Sasha speaks.

"Graham?"

"Shit," Ethan mutters.

Graham doesn't look at them. He continues to face me. As if both of our lives aren't falling apart around us, Graham calmly says to me, "Would you like me to walk with you downstairs?"

I nod.

"Graham!" Sasha says his name like she has a right to be angry at him for being here.

Graham and I both stand up. Neither of us look toward Ethan's apartment. Graham has a tight grip on my hand as he leads me to the elevator.

She's right behind us, then next to us as we wait for the

elevator. She's on the other side of Graham, pulling on his shirtsleeve. He squeezes my hand a little harder, so I squeeze his back, letting him know we can do this without a scene. Just walk onto the elevator and leave.

When the doors open, Graham ushers me on first and then he steps on. He doesn't leave room for Sasha to step on with us. He blocks the doorway and we're forced to face the direction of the doors. The direction of Sasha. He hits the button for the lobby and when the doors begin to close, I finally look up.

I notice two things.

1) Ethan is no longer in the hallway and his apartment door is closed.
2) Sasha is so much prettier than me. Even when she's crying.

The doors close and it's a long, quiet ride to the bottom. Graham doesn't let go of my hand and we don't speak, but we also don't cry. We walk quietly out of the elevator and across the lobby. When we reach the door, Vincent holds it open for us, looking at us both with apology in his eyes. Graham pulls out his wallet and gives Vincent a handful of bills. "Thanks for the apartment number," Graham says.

Vincent nods and takes the cash. When his eyes meet mine, they're swimming in apology. I give Vincent a hug since I'll likely never see him again.

Once Graham and I are outside, we just stand on the sidewalk, dumbfounded. I wonder if the world looks different to him now because it certainly looks different to me. The sky, the trees, the people who pass us on the sidewalk. Everything seems slightly more disappointing than it did before I walked into Ethan's building.

"You want me to hail you a cab?" he finally says.

"I drove. That's my car," I say, pointing across the street.

He glances back up at the apartment building. "I want to get out of here before she makes it down." He looks genuinely worried, like he can't face her at all right now.

At least Sasha is trying. She followed Graham all the way to the elevator while Ethan just walked back inside his apartment and closed his door.

Graham looks back at me, his hands shoved in his jacket pockets. I wrap my coat tightly around myself. There's not much left to say other than goodbye.

"Goodbye, Graham."

His stare is flat, like he's not even in this moment. He backs up a step. Two steps. Then he spins and starts walking in the other direction.

I look back at the apartment building, just as Sasha bursts through the doors. Vincent is behind her, staring at me. He waves at me, so I lift a hand and wave back to him. We both know it's a goodbye wave, because I'm never stepping foot inside Ethan's apartment building again. Not even for whatever stuff of mine litters his apartment. I'd rather him just throw it all away than face him again.

Sasha looks left and then right, hoping to find Graham. She doesn't. She just finds me and it makes me wonder if she even knows who I am. Did Ethan tell her he's supposed to get married next month? Did he tell her we just spoke on the phone this morning and he told me he's counting down the seconds until he gets to call me his wife? Does she know when I sleep over at Ethan's apartment that he refuses to shower without me? Did he tell her the sheets he just fucked her on were an engagement gift from my sister?

Does she know when Ethan proposed to me, he cried when I said yes?

She must not realize this or she wouldn't have thrown away her relationship with a guy who impressed me more in one hour than Ethan did in four years.